Let's Sing a Lullaby with the BRAVE COWBOY

by Jan Thomas

BEACH LANE BOOKS · New York London Toronto Sydney New Delhi

It's time
for little cows
to rest their heads.
It's time
for little cows
to go to bed.
It's time
for little cows
to sleep so tight.
It's time
for us to say . . .

Ee

eeek!

Is that a
HUGE
HAIRY
SPIDER
over there?!!

It's just a FLOWER, Cowboy!

Oh.

Well, let's try that lullaby again, shall we?

It's time
for little cows
to rest their heads.
It's time
for little cows
to go to bed.
It's time
for little cows
to sleep so tight.
It's time
for us to say . . .

Ee

eeek!

Is that a
SLIMY
SLITHERING
SNAKE
right there?!!

It's just a STICK, Cowboy.
Oh.

But is there a
LARGE
LUMBERING
BEAR
behind me?!!

It's just ME, Cowboy.
Oh.

Hey, I see how this works.
It may LOOK like a
HUGE SHAGGY GRAY WOLF
over there. . . .

Grrrrrrrr.
Grrrrrrrrr.
And it may SOUND like one too!

Eeeeek!

But it's probably just a BIG GIANT BUNNY RABBIT. Right?

No, Cowboy, it's a
WOLF!

Um, do wolves like lullabies?

Like ’em? We **LOVE** ’em!!!

Well, all righty then!
It's time
for us
to rest our heads.
It's time
for us
to go to bed.
It's time
for us
to sleep so tight.
It's time
for us to saaaaaay . . .